For Natalie - *MM*
For Marina - *PN*

Series reading consultant: Prue Goodwin,
Reading and Language Information Centre,
University of Reading

Orchard Books
338 Euston Road, London NW1 3BH
Orchard Books Australia
Hachette Children's Books
Level 17/207 Kent Street, Sydney, NSW 2000
This text was first published in Great Britain in the form
of a gift collection called *First Fairy Tales*,
illustrated by Selina Young, in 1994
This edition first published in Great Britain in hardback in 2002
First paperback publication 2003
Text © Margaret Mayo 2002
Illustrations © Philip Norman 2002
The rights of Margaret Mayo to be identified as the author and
Philip Norman to be identified as the illustrator have been
asserted by them in accordance with the
Copyright, Designs and Patents Act, 1988.
A CIP catalogue record for this book is available from the British Library
ISBN 1 84121 132 X (hardback)
ISBN 1 84121 144 3 (paperback)
1 3 5 7 9 10 8 6 4 2 (hardback)
5 7 9 10 8 6 (paperback)
Printed in China

FIRST FAIRY TALES
Sleeping Beauty

Margaret Mayo ⭐ Philip Norman

ORCHARD BOOKS

Once upon a time, there was a king and queen. When their baby daughter was born, they were so happy, they decided to have a party.

They invited all their family, their friends *and* all the fairies in the land.

Now, there were thirteen fairies altogether, but the king and queen only invited twelve. They completely forgot about the thirteenth…

It was a splendid party. There were gold dishes piled high with delicious food for everyone.

When everyone had finished eating, the fairies gathered round the baby's cradle, and they each made a magic wish.

"The princess shall be beautiful," said the first.

"And happy," said the second.
"And kind," said the third.
And so they went on.

The princess was to be brave and clever. She was to have a sweet singing voice and light dancing feet.

But then…just as the twelfth fairy was about to make her wish, in came the thirteenth!

She was furious because she had not been invited to the party.

"Here is my wish," she said. "When the princess is sixteen, she will prick her finger on a spindle and die!"

And with that, the thirteenth fairy vanished.

Then, the twelfth fairy said,
"I cannot change all of the wicked
fairy's powerful magic. So the
princess *will* prick her finger...

but she will not die. She will fall
asleep for a hundred years."

The king and queen thanked
the twelfth fairy for her wish, but
they were sad. They did not want
their daughter to sleep for a
hundred years.

The king and queen ordered
that every spindle and spinning-wheel
in the land must be chopped up and
burnt. Then, they thought their
daughter was safe.

The years passed, and the
princess grew up. She was very
beautiful and clever. She was
everything the fairies had wished
her to be.

Then, on her sixteenth birthday, the princess was exploring the castle, and she found a little room at the top of a tall tower.

In the room was an old woman,
sitting by a spinning-wheel.

"What are you doing?" asked
the princess.

"I am spinning," said the old woman, who was really the wicked thirteenth fairy. "Would you like to try?"

"Oh, yes!" said the princess. And she sat down by the spinning-wheel.

But, as soon as she touched the
spindle, the sharp point pricked
her finger and she fell asleep.
Then, the old woman vanished.

At the same moment, the king
and queen,

the servants,

and the cats and dogs

all fell asleep.

Even the fire stopped burning and the roasting meat stopped sizzling. Everything slept.

A hedge of wild roses grew up around the castle. It grew and grew, until the castle was almost hidden.

One hundred years passed, and then a prince came riding by and saw the top of a tower behind the hedge of roses.

"How strange," he said. "I never knew there was a castle here."

He jumped off his horse and lifted his sword to cut a way through the hedge. But, as soon as the sword touched a branch, a path opened up.

The prince entered the castle and walked from room to room. Imagine his surprise, finding everyone and everything fast asleep!

At last, he entered a little room at the top of a tall tower, and he saw the sleeping princess.

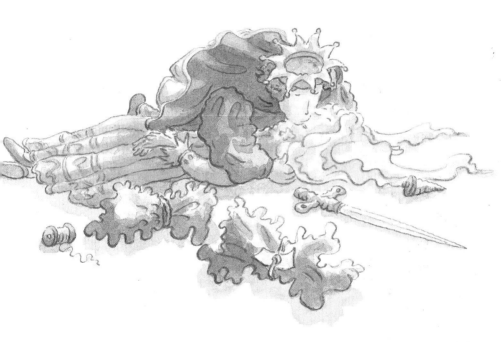

She looked so beautiful that he bent down and kissed her.

The spell was broken! The princess opened her eyes, and everybody and everything in the castle awoke.

The king yawned, the queen blinked, the cats had a good stretch and the dogs wagged their tails.

The servants began to work, the fire began to flame and the roasting meat began to sizzle.

A hundred years had not changed anyone or anything.

And, then, the beautiful princess married the prince who had woken her from such a long, deep sleep.

FIRST FAIRY TALES

by Margaret Mayo

Illustrated by Philip Norman

Enjoy a little more magic with these First Fairy Tales:

❏ Cinderella	1 84121 150 8	£3.99
❏ Hansel and Gretel	1 84121 148 6	£3.99
❏ Jack and the Beanstalk	1 84121 146 X	£3.99
❏ Sleeping Beauty	1 84121 144 3	£3.99
❏ Rumpelstiltskin	1 84121 152 4	£3.99
❏ Snow White	1 84121 154 0	£3.99

Colour Crackers

by Rose Impey

Illustrated by Shoo Rayner

Have you read any Colour Crackers?

❏ A Birthday for Bluebell	1 84121 228 8	£3.99
❏ Hot Dog Harris	1 84121 232 6	£3.99
❏ Tiny Tim	1 84121 240 7	£3.99
❏ Too Many Babies	1 84121 242 3	£3.99

and many other titles.

First Fairy Tales and Colour Crackers are available from all good
bookshops, or can be ordered direct from the publisher:
Orchard Books, PO BOX 29, Douglas IM99 1BQ
Credit card orders please telephone 01624 836000
or fax 01624 837033
or e-mail: bookshop@enterprise.net for details.

To order please quote title, author and ISBN
and your full name and address.
Cheques and postal orders should be
made payable to 'Bookpost plc'.
Postage and packing is FREE within the UK
(overseas customers should add £1.00 per book).

Prices and availability are subject to change.